Too Many Frogs!

Sandy Asher

illustrations by

Keith Graves

SCHOLASTIC INC.

New York Toronto London Auckland Sydney
Mexico City New Delhi Hong Kong Buenos Aires

R abbit lived by himself in
the hollow of an old tree.
   He cooked for himself.
   He tidied up after himself.
   And at the end of each and every
day, he read himself a story.
   It was a simple way of life—
no fuss, no clutter.
   And Rabbit liked it.

But one rainy evening, he heard a knock-knockety-knocking at his door.

"It's Froggie!" croaked a deep voice. "Don't care for this storm."

Rabbit opened the door. "I was about to read myself a story."

"Love to listen!" Froggie cried, and hopped right inside. "Don't mind, do you?"

"I suppose not," Rabbit said.

So Froggie listened while Rabbit
read his story.

"Well done!" he cheered when Rabbit
had finished. "Storm's ended, too.
Thanks for your kindness.
Toodle-oo!"

The next evening, as usual, Rabbit finished dinner, tidied up, and sat down to read himself a story.

But before he could begin, he heard another knock-knockety-knocking at his door.

"It's Froggie!" croaked the same deep voice.

Rabbit opened the door. "I was about to read myself a story."

"I know!" Froggie cried, and hopped right inside. "Love to listen! But first, let's fix ourselves a snack—or three! Don't mind, do you?"

"I suppose not," Rabbit said.

So Froggie hopped—
and popped—
and whipped—
and flipped—
and mixed—
and fixed a snack. Or three.

Too much fuss! Rabbit thought.

But Froggie listened while Rabbit read his story.

"Well done!" he cheered when Rabbit had finished. "Snack's gone, too. Thanks for your kindness.
                    Toodle-oo!"

"Yo ho ho," said the Purple Pig Pirate. "I am so hungry I could eat my boots! And he did.

The next evening, Rabbit finished dinner, tidied up, and sat down to read himself another story.

But before he could begin, there was that same knock-knockety-knocking at his door.

"It's Froggie!" croaked the familiar voice.

Rabbit opened the door. "I was about to read—," he began.

"I know!" Froggie cried, and hopped right inside. "About to read yourself a story. Love to listen! But first, let's get ourselves all comfy-cozy. Don't mind, do you?"

"I suppose not," said Rabbit.

So Froggie fluffed—
and puffed—
and mooshed—
and smooshed—
and piled up billows—
of pillows.

Too much clutter, Rabbit thought.

But Froggie listened while Rabbit read his story.

"Well done!" he cheered when Rabbit had finished. "Bedtime, too! Thanks for your kindness.

Toodle-oo!"

The next evening, Rabbit finished dinner, tidied up, and sat down to read himself a new story.

But before he could begin, there was that knock-knockety-knocking again!

"It's Froggie!"

Rabbit opened the door.

"I know!" Froggie cried before Rabbit could say a single word. "You were about to read yourself a story. Love to listen! But first, meet the family! Been telling them all about you and your stories. Love to join us! Don't mind, do you?"

Rabbit looked at Froggie's family, big frogs and little frogs, dozens and dozens, all wearing T-shirts: FROG FAMILY REUNION.

Too many frogs! he thought. Too much fuss! Too much clutter!

"But I DO mind, Froggie," he said at last.

"You do?" Froggie asked.

"I never invited you in," Rabbit explained. "I never invited you to fix a snack. I never invited you to get all comfy-cozy. And I never invited your family to join you. So I do mind. Very much indeed."

"Uh-oh!" croaked Froggie.
"This will never do. Thanks for
your kindness.

Toodle-oo."

Alone at last, Rabbit sat down to read himself a story.
For one anxious moment, he waited for a knock-knockety-knocking at his door.
It never came.

"Don't mind, do you?" he asked himself, with a chuckle.
"Most certainly not," he answered himself, and began to read.
It was a good story.

But something was missing.
Snacks make a good story better, he thought.
So he fixed himself a snack and read on.
It was a very good story.

But something was missing.
Pillows make a good story
better, he thought.
So he fluffed himself
a pillow and read on.
It was an exceptionally
good story.
But something was
still missing. . . .

Rabbit blinked once. He blinked twice. And then he sighed.

It's Froggie, he told himself, at last. He loves to listen.

Rabbit opened his door.

There sat Froggie and his family, waiting patiently to say they were sorry.

"Never meant to be rude," Froggie said. "Brought you a T-shirt: FROG FAMILY REUNION."

"Thank you," Rabbit said. "I was about to read a story. Would you like to join me?"

"Love to listen!" cried the frogs.

And in they all hopped, big frogs and little frogs, dozens and dozens.
Rabbit offered them a snack—or three—
and helped them fluff their pillows.
Then every frog listened while Rabbit read a story.

"Well done!" they cheered
when he had finished.
   So many frogs! Rabbit
thought. So much fuss! So
much clutter!
   It was a different way of life.
And Rabbit liked it.

For Elizabeth and Judy Baughman,
and in memory of Ron

—S.A.

For Tambo

—K.G.

ISBN 0-439-85571-3

Text copyright © 2005 by Sandy Asher.
Illustrations copyright © 2005 by Keith Graves. All rights reserved.
Published by Scholastic Inc., 557 Broadway, New York, NY 10012,
by arrangement with Philomel Books, an imprint of Penguin Putnam
Books for Young Readers, a division of Penguin Group (USA) Inc.
SCHOLASTIC and associated logos are trademarks and/or registered
trademarks of Scholastic Inc.

12 11 10 9 8 7 6 5 4 3 2 1   6 7 8 9 10 11/0

Printed in the U.S.A.   40

First Scholastic printing, April 2006

Design by Gina DiMassi

The text is set in Klepto.

The art was created using acrylic paint, inks, and pencil
color on illustration board.